WHO AM I

A novel by

Natasha Simmons

Who Am I

ISBN-13: 978-0996712705
ISBN-10: 0996712704

Published by Thomas Publishing

Who Am I

To the loves of my life, Kori, Dorian and Kendall.

Love, Mom

And to Elvira Phoenix Martin, who never stops believing in me. Thank you, for without your encouragement my journey would have been very different.

Who Am I

The journey inside the mirror is often the longest and most difficult of all.

CHAPTER 1

"Do you know why you're in my office?"

"Because Shay Jones called me a bitch."

I can tell by the way she raises her eyebrow that she doesn't expect me to use *that* word, but I don't care. She shouldn't have asked.

She sighs heavily as if she doesn't feel like dealing with this on a Friday afternoon, and sits behind her desk. She pulls a referral from the small stack tucked into a slot of trays. Most teachers' desks are a pile of chaos, but not Mrs. Martin's, everything has its place and everything is always in place. I've never even seen a stray paperclip.

Who Am I

I find myself looking at the pictures on her shelves. In the pictures Mrs. Martin looks like a normal person. She's smiling pretty with two little girls and a man—her kids and husband, I suppose.

She has a family?

For some reason I can't imagine her picking up toys and wiping up the constant messes kids make.

"And are you?"

"Huh?"

"Huh?" She repeats in that tone I hate.

"Ma'am?" I correct myself. She seems slightly satisfied. "Am I what?"

"A bitch?"

I can't help the giggle that shoots out of my mouth when I hear her curse.

"Oh, that's funny?" Her brows slowly inch up on her forehead again before she pushes me for a reply. "So?"

She's really expecting me to answer her?

She leans back in her chair and stares at me. I guess she is.

"Noo-o!" The word scrapes across my tongue in two syllables like a hoarse whine.

"So why are you reacting to something that doesn't even apply to you?"

"I ain't no bitch! She got me messed up. That ain't me.!" She looks at me like she's daring me to say it again. I look out of the window.

Even to my own ears, I sound out of character. Why do they push us to behave like we don't have any sense? My mom would kill me if she heard me talking this way.

She sighs again and corrects me. "That *isn't* me…Not ain't."

I look at her and try not to roll my eyes.

"That *isn't* me." I repeat, mockingly.

This is my third time in Mrs. Martin's office this year for running off at the mouth with someone. I am tired of her and I know good and well she's tired of me.

"So who are you?"

I look at her then back towards the window so she can't see me rolling my eyes. There's a bird flying by. I see it fly off into the distance, swooping and gliding like it doesn't have a care in the world.

How does it feel to swoop in the air like that?

8

"I asked you a question." She says, breaking me from my bird watching.

I hold my head high and stare right back at her. "I'm Tameka Nicole Cummings."

I say it clearly—triumphantly.

Nah…take that!

"And who is that, exactly?" She asks, leaning forward in her chair, not the least bit impressed by my declaration.

This lady is getting on my last nerve. Why can't she be like other assistant principals and just punish me and send me on my way? Mrs. Martin has to get all up in people's business.

"Huh?" I just told her.

That look again.

"I mean, Ma'am?"

Who Am I

"Who *is* Tameka Nicole Cummings?"

"Whatcha mean?"

"I mean, who are you?"

I'm confused. What's she talking about?

"I'm me."

"So, who are you? What are you made of?"

I just stare at her. *What am I made of?* No one has ever asked me that before.

Mrs. Martin stands and walks to her file cabinet. I roll my eyes. She's getting my parent contact info…I know the drill.

"You seem to know what or who you're not, so who exactly is Tameka?" When she knows I'm not going to say anything, she continues. "If you don't know who you are, then maybe you are what Shay called you."

10

"I ain't no bi—" She shoots a look at me. "I'm not that."

"How do you know?"

"I know."

Did I say I was tired of her?

She sighs again, sits back in her chair, and stabs buttons on the phone with her pen. The rest is the same old routine, though instead of giving me detention or in-school-suspension, she tells me I need to stay after school every Monday with her until I can tell her who I am. Mrs. Martin is known for coming up with something crazy just to torture us. And this seems like student agony at its finest.

At first I'm pissed, but then I realize I won't have to stay after school at all. I just have to tell her what she wants to hear. I roll my eyes and I don't try to hide it. She thrusts the white hall pass out to me, letting me know she's done with our little session. I take it and walk out. Before the door closes, I hear her sigh… *with pity*.

I hate that sound.

It makes me feel invisible—like I don't matter.

I matter.

Don't I?

I think about *that* question as well as the one Mrs. Martin asked, all weekend. I find myself staring in my bathroom mirror trying to figure out who I see and what I'm all about. Right now, all I see is a plain light brown face, brown eyes, and a ponytail, because I'm too lazy to fool with all of this hair every morning. So up in a ponytail it goes.

How do other girls do it?

Maybe they take time with their hair because it displays a specific image of who they are. Maybe they know for certain that they matter. I wonder what my image says about me.

CHAPTER 2

It's Monday after school. I stand outside of Mrs. Martin's door with my backpack at my feet. I hope she doesn't notice the hole in the knee of my jeans. I've made it through the entire school day without a teacher saying anything to me. I kick the floor softly with the toe of my favorite white Chucks, a little nervous. I still have no answers.

"Tameka, girl, you gon' miss the bus." My friend, Trina, yells as she runs toward the front of the school. She must've had to run at gym, because her hair is scattered all over her head. Clearly she doesn't know this, because she prides herself on keeping her hair completely tamed at all times and perfect. I self-consciously smooth mine down and tighten my ponytail.

"My mom's picking me up today."

I lie.

I don't know how I'm getting home. I didn't plan on staying after school, but I haven't come up with anything to tell Mrs. Martin. I think about getting on the bus anyway, but I kind of want to see what she'll make me do when I don't have anything to tell her.

"Come in, Tameka."

Does she have x-ray vision or something? How does she know I'm standing at the door? I walk in, drop my backpack on the floor and slump myself into the chair without her usual invitation to sit.

"Well?"

I pretend I'm trying to fix the zipper on my jacket, but she knows I'm stalling.

"Who are you?" I hear her ask.

I don't look up. I hear her stand and the rustle of something as she pulls it from her file cabinet drawer. "Come on."

I look up, startled. She's typing in a text as she moves toward the door.

"Huh? I mean, Ma'am?"

"Come on." She pulls out her keys and places her fingers on the light switch.

What's she talking about? Go where? My mom doesn't even know I'm staying after school. It's a good thing she's working late. Maybe Mrs. Martin is going to leave me with another teacher or with the custodians to do some work.

Who Am I

She looks at me pointedly, still sitting in the chair. I guess I'm taking too long to get up and follow her. She ignores the smacking sound my lips make to show my displeasure. I roll my eyes, grab the handle of my backpack and drag it in front of the chair as I slowly lift from the seat.

I follow Mrs. Martin from the office and down the corridor. Her heels echo loudly through the empty halls. I finally sling the backpack over one shoulder, because I'm having a hard time keeping up with her. Apparently the sky-high heels are like her track shoes.

She must be in a hurry to dump me off somewhere. We head towards the cafeteria. I resign to the fact that I will have to scrape gum or pick up trash, but when we pass the cafeteria, it's clean and empty of anyone. We pass by it.

Who Am I

When we walk out to the teacher's parking lot, a gust of wind pushes me hard. The sky is dark and angry and it smells like it's going to pour at any second. My friends think I'm crazy when I tell them I can smell the rain coming.

But I can.

It smells sad and refreshing at the same time. Maybe I *am* crazy.

I slow. She turns to look at me then up at the sky.

"Come on, Tameka, the sky is going to open any minute."

I know that. What does she want me to do? She waves her hand rapidly for me to follow her. So I do. At that moment, fat drops of water splash on my arm. The sky is indeed opening. I follow her as she runs to a small blue car. The rain is coming down hard and fast now, and we both start screaming like it's made of acid or something.

Pouring rain makes people too trusting and impulsive—me included. I don't have time to question whether I should get in her car or not. I open the door and jump in the front seat. I'm so focused on getting in and getting the door closed as quickly as possible that my backpack gets jammed between the door and the seat.

My mind is all over the place. I can't help but think about my hair and the massive puff it will become from getting wet.

The rain came on us so suddenly, as it often does in early springtime in Houston, that it doesn't occur to me to pull on the hood of my jacket. In the meantime I'm still yanking on my backpack handle, but it won't budge.

"Open the door!" Mrs. Martin screeches.

I do, soaking my entire right side in the process. The bag is finally free and the door closed. I sit back and look over at Mrs. Martin. The sound of the rain is muffled from within the car. She looks at me. I stare back at her. Everything has happened so quickly. The rain, the dash to the car, and the backpack lodged in the door.

Laughter erupts from us both. I mean a loud girly laughter that explodes out of nowhere and makes me grab my belly. It's a strange sound that contrasts with the violent weather outside of the car.

As it settles, an awkward silence rises between us.

Who Am I

I suddenly remember I'm sitting in Mrs. Martin's car and I have no idea why. The rain pounding hard against the windows and the angry rumble of the thunder, do nothing to set me at ease. It's like a weird omen or a bad horror spoof.

The wipers swing wildly, doing little to dispel the water rushing like a waterfall on her window. I look out the passenger window and resist an urge to draw a butterfly on the foggy glass. She starts the car and my eyes fly towards her. We are leaving the school. We are really leaving in Mrs. Martin's car. Where is she taking me? This was not part of the deal.

"My mom doesn't know I'm staying after school." I confess in a panic.

"I told her last night when I saw her at the book club." She says, much too easily.

21

What?

Book club?

My mom is in a book club with some of her good friends. I hadn't met them all, but they hang out regularly. What does this mean? Does my mom know Mrs. Martin?

"You're in my mom's book club?" My voice cracks, still a bit raw from laughing hysterically.

"Yes."

I don't know what she sees on my face, but I'm sure I look as if someone has just told me Tupac is still alive.

She frowns. "What?"

"Ummm…nothing." I look at the fogged window again and then quickly turn back towards her. "What'd she say?"

"She said that was fine. She has to work, but will probably be home by the time we're done."

Done? Done with what? The question burns my tongue, but I hold it there. I want her to think I don't care, but honestly, I do. She shifts the car into gear, back out of the slot, and head towards the street that's beginning to flood slightly.

Wait! Something doesn't sit right with me. She'd talked to my mom last night, which is a new development. This means my mom has the inside scoop on what's going on with me at school. Not that I'm a walking terror or anything like that, but I tend to get into trouble because I can't keep my mouth shut when I feel like someone is disrespecting me or my friends—like now. Mrs. Marin took for granted that I wouldn't have an answer for her today.

"So you just assumed I wouldn't be able to answer your question?" I shot at her.

Her eyes are focusing on the road through the clear spot on the windshield. Her defrost is clearing the fogged window, but the rain is still making it difficult to see.

"I didn't assume anything, Tameka." She doesn't take her eyes off the road. "I simply saw your mom and told her about the deal we'd made." She glances at me then back on the road. "I texted her before I left the office, to let her know you're with me and that I'll bring you home later."

"Oh." I mumble.

The new song by Beyoncé is on the radio.

I love that song!

Just as I thought it, she says it and begins snapping her fingers. "That's my jam!" She announces before she starts singing *my* favorite song. I look at her and then turn away. I fish my ear buds and phone out of the side pocket of my backpack, plug the buds into my phone and stick them in my ears.

"Don't you just love this song?" She asks, beaming at me like we're friends.

How dare she like the same song I like! I look away and pretend I'm so into the song I'm listening to that I can't hear her question.

We look like we are heading towards the mall.

Why is she taking me there?

Instead of going to the mall, we turn into a shopping center. She parks in front of a copy and print store. I'd come here once with my mom when we were picking up my dad's business cards.

As a real estate agent, he needs to always have them on hand. My dad also works on motorcycles on the side, although it seems the real estate is the side job sometimes.

The print shop is owned by Jessica Stewart's dad and she works for him after school and on weekends.

Stuck up heifer.

She thinks just because her dad owns a few stores and they live in a large house in a gated community, that she's better than everyone else.

I live in that same community and don't act like that. She drives around in her convertible Mustang and runs around after Justin Fisher, the football quarterback, as if he leaves a trail of gold when he walks. Everybody knows he's just using her and he's cheating on her with some girl that goes to the cosmetology program on our campus.

The stupid heifer even caught him with her one day, but she's one of those girls who believes any lie a boy says, just because he smells good and looks like God carved him with his bare hands.

There's no sense in lying though, he *is* fine.

But still, she's a pretty girl. I notice how all the guys watch her walk by as she pretends not to care. The decent guys look at her, but they have enough sense to let her keep on walking by. They know what a brat she is.

The last time I was in here with my mom, Jessica pretended like she didn't know me, like we hadn't been in the same Girl Scout troupe together through seventh grade. In eighth grade, she transferred to a private school until our tenth grade year, and now that we're seniors and she has three years of private school under her belt, she suddenly can't remember that we once sang "John Jacob Jingle Hiemer Smith," around the campfire.

Rumor has it that she was kicked out of private school for flirting with a teacher, but I don't know how true that is. I don't care. We aren't friends. She can pretend she doesn't know me all she wants to. We don't even have any classes together and our worlds never mix, so oh well.

Now that I think about it, I haven't seen Jessica around school lately.

"Come on. I need your help inside." Mrs. Martin says, interrupting my thoughts.

What in the world are we going to do here? I sure hope no one sees me with this woman.

CHAPTER 3

The rain slacked to a drizzle so I'm in no jeopardy of getting soaked, but my clothes are still damp from the deluge we'd encountered earlier. I don't even want to think about my hair.

I'm sure Jessica will have something to say or better yet, a smirk on her face when I walk in. Her hair always perfected by $300 weave and weekly hair appointments.

We walk into the store.

I was wrong.

Jessica is waiting on customers behind the counter as usual but her eyes avoid meeting any gazes that are directed at her. It's the first time in my life I'm actually witnessing her appearing anything close to humble.

Is it humble I'm seeing?

More like…shame.

Jessica Stewart. The always perfectly groomed and poised girl with hair flowing down her back, trendy name-brand outfits, and usually over accessorized.

But not today.

Today her hair is free of the mid-back length weave, though still long enough to be pulled back into a plain single French braid, which she's wearing now. Her smooth dark brown face is free of makeup and she's wearing a pair of jeans and an over-sized t-shirt that does not hide her bulging belly.

She's pregnant!

And after all the times I'd watched her look down her nose at people or critique and shun other girls who'd found themselves in the same position...I want to gloat. I want to give her a pointed stare that said, "Well, well, well, look how the mighty has fallen." But I don't.

I can't.

The emptiness in her eyes tells me she already knows it. I look up at Mrs. Martin who has an unreadable expression on her face.

"Welcome to Stewart's Print 'N Copy." Jessica says, sounding like a robot.

"Hi Jessica." Mrs. Martin greets her cheerily. I'm here for my usual, but I also need some folders. I'll grab some while you gather my order. Is it ready?"

"Yes Ma'am." Her eyes are on anything, but us.

Mrs. Martin places a large envelope on the counter and leaves me.

I watch Jessica move around the counter doing nothing really. I can tell by the way her eyes are darting everywhere, but at me, that she's uncomfortable or embarrassed, I don't know which. I look around the store to see if I can spot Mrs. Martin. She's hidden among the shelves.

This is ridiculous; there's no reason for me to pretend we don't know each other.

"Hi Jessica." I say, simply, and wonder what her reply will be this time.

"Hi Tameka." My eyes widen slightly. Oh she remembers me today, but I don't make a big deal out of it.

"Your hair looks nice like that." I tell her, because I've had enough of awkward silence for one day. She stares at me, warily. "I remember when you used to braid mine like that." I add.

She doesn't say anything, just puts a few boxes on the counter. Mrs. Martin walks up and places about twenty folders with the boxes—I assume they are boxes of things she's had copied.

"I think that'll do me for today." In a softer tone, she adds, "Have you been feeling better?"

Jessica's eyes flick my way then back to Mrs. Martin, before she answers.

"Yes ma'am. The crackers helped."

"Good, Honey." Mrs. Martin pays and then turns to me. "Grab those two boxes, Tameka, and I'll get the rest. We're going to put the folders together in the workroom over there."

I feel like I'm caught up in some kind of psycho Lifetime movie.

The print shop has a little room off to the side that customers can use if it's available, to do things like spiral-bind books, staple papers, or whatever. There's a big table to spread out and sort, which is what Mrs. Martin wants my help with. There are various assignments for several different subjects, all in huge letters. There's even an assignment Mr. Fintch gave us in economics just yesterday, but the writing is blown up much larger on this piece of paper.

"What are these for?" I ask.

"Some students have a difficult time seeing the notes on the board or reading the small print on the worksheets or assignments." She finishes stuffing a folder and holds it up. "So I put these together for the students who really want them and are trying hard to keep up."

I look at the table. We have about twenty folders or more.

"Glasses don't help?" I ask.

"I'm sure they would, if they could afford them, but their parents can't afford them."

"How much do glasses cost?" I'd never had any and I don't have any siblings. I've had a few friends who wear glasses but never thought about the cost of them or the consequences if they don't have them.

"The exam can range from forty bucks to over a hundred and a pair of glasses can cost from fifty bucks, usually just for the frames, to several hundred."

"Oh." I say, quietly. I thought there were government programs that provide insurance to people who can't afford it. So I ask her about that.

"There are, but many people don't qualify, because they make too much money." She says as if this answers my question.

"Well if they make too much money, why can't they get their own insurance?" I ask.

"It's not that simple, Tameka." She stuffs the last folder and then looks back at me. "Making too much for government programs is still not enough sometimes for working people to provide all of their family's essential needs...like medical care."

"So basically what you're saying is that people who are working their butts off can't get the same help as people who don't have a job at all?"

"Bingo."

I'm floored. This makes absolutely no sense to me at all.

We place the folders in the now empty boxes.

"Well that's it. Thanks for your help. I usually have to do this all by myself. It was faster with two sets of hands."

It wasn't hard, but all the sorting was a bit tedious. It would have taken forever for Mrs. Martin to do it on her own. Except for the glasses, we didn't talk much at all. I have to admit, I thought she would grill me the entire time, but she didn't. It's kind of cool that she enlarges assignments for students. It seems to me that she does it out of her own money and on her own time.

With the folders in hand, we head to the car.

"Goodbye, Jessica." Mrs. Martin calls out over her shoulder.

"Bye, Mrs. Martin." She answers.

Just as we are reaching the door I hear Jessica's voice, it's unusually soft. "Bye, Tami." I stop and turn towards her. She looks directly at me. The first time I've seen her do that to anyone since we arrived.

We stand there taking measure of each other and just like that, I push away the stuck up Jessica, and only see the girl I knew when we were kids. Her mouth lifts at one corner slightly, for the briefest of moments.

"Bye, Jessie. Tell Mr. and Mrs. Stewart I said hello."

Sadness flashes across her face before a full smile appears and the Jessie I'd known long ago is standing there.

CHAPTER 4

The next day at lunch, I notice several of the black folders I'd stuffed, walking by my table. It makes me think about my evening with Mrs. Martin and the fact that she never asked me *the* question again. For some reason it irritates me that she never asked again. Is she just waiting for me to bring it up or does she think I'm still unable or unwilling to answer?

I see Jolisha Kenny with a folder. Everyone knows her dad is in prison and her mom is most likely on drugs. She lives with her grandmother along with her little brother and her uncle. Her uncle has done some work on our house and my dad tries to recommend him whenever he can, when people need work done on their homes.

I like Jolisha and seeing her with the folder makes me think about the cost of glasses again. It also makes me think about the print shop and Jessica Stewart.

Normally when a girl gets pregnant who goes to our school, everyone knows. The talk, whether it's true or not, spreads through the school like it has wings. Yet, no one is talking about Jessica.

Are they?

Maybe I'm the only person who doesn't know. I wonder if Trina knows. I won't ask her just in case she doesn't. For some reason I feel protective of Jessica all of a sudden.

Who Am I

The cafeteria echoes with clanking trays and a mirage of noise usually accompanied by a large group of teenagers.

"It ought to be a crime to serve this crap to us." Trina grumbles as she plops down into the chair next to mine.

She complains every day about the lunch, but every day she stands in line to get it. I slide her half of my sandwich that's left in my sandwich bag. Today it's ham and cheese. This is my routine every day.

She smiles as if it's a surprise and I pretend I don't want it, when in fact, every day I hope she comes to the table without complaint.

It never happens.

"Why don't you bring your lunch like I do?" I ask her, trying not to sound annoyed.

"Girl, my momma said she ain't buying no lunch when I can get it for free."

I had no idea Trina was on free lunch. The bus drops her off in Casper Cove. My dad would love to get his hands on a property in that neighborhood. He had, once and after the sale we took a trip to the Grand Cayman Islands.

"You get free lunch?" I whisper, trying to keep the irritation from my face and voice.

She stops chewing on the bite of *my* sandwich. I watch her face bunch in surprise and confusion. Her eyes doesn't leave mine, even though Tiffany James is cussing out her boyfriend *again,* right behind us.

"Yeah." The word pushes out from around the bread in her mouth. She narrows her eyes. "Why?" She asks, after swallowing the bite.

44

Who Am I

I want to say, "Oh girl, it's nothing" or "never mind, I'm trippin'," but I can't.

The price of school lunch is a constant topic in my house. My parents often are scraping money together to come up with enough for me to buy lunch at school. It's just this year I resigned to bringing a sandwich every day because my mom works part-time in a deli and gets to bring home deli-meat ends sometimes.

Yes, we live in a nice neighborhood, but my parents bought the house when the real estate market was doing well. Now, we don't have a lot of money for the extra things we used to have and do.

I don't want it to, but it bothers me knowing Trina lives in a nicer neighborhood than me, wears all the latest styles, gets her hair and nails done often, and yet here she is eating half of a sandwich made with my mom's work scraps, because I feel sorry for her.

"But you live in Casper Cove." I state flatly.

"And?" She places the rest of the sandwich on the lunch tray, not caring that gravy from the mashed potatoes is getting all over it.

Do I have an *and*?

"And, how can you get free lunch if you live in Casper Cove?"

Trina's stare slaps me hard across the face, but I don't flinch and meet it with one of my own.

"Do you have a problem with people who get free lunch?"

Of course I do not. I know there are people who genuinely can't afford to pay for the lunch at school, but you can look at them and tell they should get it.

46

Can't you?

Do I have it all wrong?

I want to look at the people sitting around me, but I don't want Trina to think...

I don't know what I want Trina to think, but I can't look away. I've known Trina since the beginning of our senior year. She'd told me her family moved from somewhere in Illinois here to Houston, but she never said why.

Before I can answer her question, she picks up her tray. "I never took you for one of those bougie bitches we talk about." She flings the words at me as she stands and stomps away.

Her words sting.

"Trina!" I finally manage to yell at her retreating back. I watch her dump the contents of her tray and storm out to the patio.

What's wrong with me asking her that?

The conversation got out of hand, way too quickly.

I can feel people staring at me but I concentrate on gathering my trash.

"What's wrong with Trina?"

I roll my eyes.

China Lewis.

We've quietly hated each other for most of our lives. Mostly because she's always trying to be the teacher's pet gerbil and I'm the one who gets much better grades than she does.

"Now if I told you that, China, it wouldn't be a secret anymore." China has a large, round, brown face that's almost pretty, but not quite, though you can't tell her that. If she wasn't on the cheer squad, I'm convinced the rest of her would be as big and round as her face.

I lean in close to her and whisper. "And we know how much you *love* secrets." I stress the word "love." Her eyes narrow and she nervously looks around before she throws out a laugh that is as fake as her relationship with her so-called "boyfriend," Scott.

She doesn't know it but I'd spotted her kissing Sabrina Sells by the bathrooms when I went to my cousin Mike's football game in Beaumont last year. I guess she figured since our school wasn't playing that night, and it was in a town over an hour away from

Houston, that she wouldn't be seen with her *girlfriend*.

Everyone knows Sabrina is gay, but I guess China

hasn't quite embraced the idea yet, and is still hiding in

the closet.

I have to admit, I am a bit impressed with

China, because to my knowledge, no one knows about

Sabrina and her—so kudos to her for being able to

keep her business to herself.

I don't need to say anything else to her.

Apparently my reference to secrets does the trick,

because her big round face and behind is bumping into

chairs and people trying to get away from me. I roll my

eyes. (It's becoming a habit lately.) That's her

business. I just wanted her out of my face.

Who Am I

I throw my trash away and head to the library

until the bell rings, wondering what's happened to the

life I had just last week.

CHAPTER 5

The following Monday I was let off the hook; Mrs. Martin had a doctor's appointment. I wasn't quite sure how I felt about not meeting with her.

Was I ready to answer the question?

Could I answer it?

Today is the Friday after the Monday she missed. She wants to meet today because next Monday we'll have the big talent show.

Who am I?

Why did she have to ask me that?

I know that in a few months I will be headed off to college, currently as a general studies major. I guess that makes sense; I don't even know who I am right now. How am I supposed to determine what I want to be for the rest of my life?

Who am I?

Apparently I'm a girl who doesn't like to see people get free lunch when they don't deserve it. But even that bothers me. Who am I to determine who deserves it or not?

It's been nearly two weeks and Trina still hasn't bothered to talk to me. She's been actively avoiding me, which leaves me to eat lunch alone most of the time. At this late stage of high school, phantom lunch seats and table assignments have long been set. I've never really even paid attention to the other people who sat with us.

Yeah, of course I have other people to talk to throughout the day, but we have superficial conversations. I guess I don't have any real friends.

Was Trina my friend?

It really should bother me that we haven't talked in a while, but it really doesn't. I guess that makes sense too. How can I be close to anyone when I'm not close enough to myself to really know me?

Urgh…

It's all so frustrating.

What will I tell Mrs. Martin?

Standing outside of her door again, I look up and down the hallway—empty. Her office is near the middle of the main hallway, right before the main office. For a split second, I think about ditching, but I really don't have anything else to do, plus I need to ask her how I'm supposed to answer her question.

What exactly does she want from me?

I pull the backpack off my shoulder and let it rest on the floor while I stand at her door. Soon her sixth sense will kick in and she'll tell me to come in.

How does she always know when I'm standing here?

I look around for cameras. There are a few, so maybe she *is* watching me stand here.

I take a deep breath and decide to knock, but right on cue, I hear her.

"Tameka!"

Why does she sound pissed?

I roll my eyes. Here we go again.

She calls again, but this time she sounds distressed; my name is nearly a plea. I walk in and when my eyes meet her I immediately know there's something wrong. Tears squeeze from her tightly shut eyes.

What the hell!

"Mrs. Martin?" I whisper, not sure what to say or do.

"Can you drive?" The words rush out of her in almost a sob.

"Mrs. Martin, are you ok? Is there—"

"Can you drive?" She cuts me off. Her eyes glazed with pain and something else. Something that makes my heart race—fear.

Whoa!

I'm stunned, momentarily stupefied. The fearless, no nonsense, Mrs. Martin looks scared to death.

"Tameka!" She yells again.

"Uh…I…can… Yes!" The words stumble out. She needs my help. "Yes Ma'am. I can drive." I reply more confidently.

Some of the tension eases from her face.

"What is it, Mrs. Martin? What's wrong?"

"Do you think you can drive me to the emergency room?"

The emergency room?

Oh no! I look towards the hallway and know it's probably still empty.

"Tameka!"

"Yes!" I don't mean to yell, but she startled me."

She eases from the seat clutching her stomach.

"Get my purse from the bottom drawer of the file cabinet. I rush to get it. I also grab her leather satchel she keeps her papers in. A thin smile touches her lips.

"The car keys are in the side pocket of my purse."

The pale yellow leather bag matches the strappy heeled sandals she's wearing. She is a snazzy dresser—I have to give her that.

"Do you want me to call someone? Your husband?" This whole episode is so far out of my league that I can't think straight. Why hasn't she called her husband to pick her up? Do I even know how to get to the hospital *and* without killing us in Houston traffic? I've had my license for two years, but this traffic can intimidate the best of drivers.

"He has the girls at his mother's in San Antonio. They won't be home 'til Sunday."

She takes a few deep breaths and we start towards the hallway.

No one…

Not a custodian, a teacher…no one is around. They are all probably in the auditorium getting ready for the talent show on Monday.

We make it to her car without incident. It's not the same car I rode in with her before. It's a fairly new and very nice, white BMW. When I look confused, she tells me it was in the shop last week.

I rush over and try to help Mrs. Martin ease into the passenger seat and then I run back to the driver's side and slip in. And even though my heart and nerves are in overdrive, it's difficult not to notice how I just seem to melt into the plush cream colored leather.

Oh my.

She tells me how to adjust the seat. I hurry to do it and then ease the car out of the nearly empty parking lot onto the street.

The dashboard is lit up like the cockpit of a space shuttle. I find the gauge to measure my speed so I don't get us pulled over and cruise towards the intersection

Oh yeah…this is smooth.

My mom's Toyota is ok, but this, I can get used to this. I almost smile until I hear the pain and panic in Mrs. Martin's words.

"Turn left at the stop sign."

"What's wrong Mrs. Martin?"

"Cramps." She replies, through gritted teeth.

Cramps?

I get cramps too, but they never send me to the hospital.

"Ok. I'll get you there." There's more to this, I'm sure.

She nods her head, tight-lipped. I watch a lone tear lose its hold on her lower lash and silently stream down her cheek. This is bad. This is really, really bad. I just know it.

I steal peeks of her as we drive. The closer we get to the hospital, the more she cries. Her pain nearly chokes me. I feel so useless.

I find myself repeating the same words over and over in my head—*she must be ok—she must be ok—she must be ok...*

"We're almost there." I try to reassure her.

"Ok." She whispers. Her eyes are shut tight. I wonder briefly, if she's afraid of my driving. "You're doing great, Tameka."

Yes, I'm getting her there—hopefully in one piece. I feel strong, more confident. I'm doing something to help. I'm getting her there.

I pull—or rather, screech the car in front of the doors that read "EMERGENCY." I jump out and run over to Mrs. Martin's side. She's still clutching her stomach and keening softly when I open the car door.

The moment I see it, I know immediately what's happening, but pray I'm wrong. Please let me be wrong.

It's just like on TV, one of those sad Lifetime movies I've watched with my mom, and I'm sure she knows what's happened also. The defeat in her watery gaze seem to see right through me.

I wonder how long she'd known. Is that why she went to the doctor, Monday? How far along is she? So many questions run through my head, but none of them can make any of this nightmare go away.

Calm penetrates me like the warmth of the sun. I have to be her strength.

"Sit here a moment, Mrs. Martin. Let me get help."

She nods without really recognizing my presence.

They took her back somewhere behind the closed doors fifteen minutes ago. The waiting room is suffocating. I know there are other people around me, but I see and hear none of them. All I can see is the widening pool of blood in Mrs. Martin's lap. I'm afraid got her here too late.

My fear is confirmed when a sickening wail pierces the quiet of the waiting area, and I know that sound will haunt me for the rest of my life.

Her screams of grief are inconsolable. They seem to go on forever. I slam my hands over my ears and run out of the hospital, nearly colliding with a janitor's cart.

I choke on the sobs that will not come, trying to rid my lungs of the stale waiting room air. My ears still ring with Mrs. Martin's cries. I feel like I'm trapped inside a glass box, unable to move, unable to get away from Mrs. Martin's pain.

STOP! STOP! STOP! STOP!

I plead with the sound. With my back pressed against the rough brick of the hospital, I sink to the ground feeling as useless as I had before.

I want to help her.

How can I help her now? My mind whirls trying to come up with something that I can do, some way I can help. I need to do something besides just sit here and then I remember the cart I nearly tripped over.

I run back into the hospital, snatch the roll of paper off the cart, and grab a bottle of spray cleaner.

Tears burn my face as I rub viciously on the leather seats. I just feel like, if I can remove all traces of blood, it will erase the last hour…it will erase the reality that a life was lost here.

CHAPTER 6

My mom shakes me gently awake. I stretch, trying to rid myself of the stiffness sleeping in a chair has caused.

"Com'on, Honey." She encourages.

"Mom?" I'm confused.

"I've come to take you home, Baby."

"Mrs. Martin…" My voice cracks. Tears immediately spring to my eyes. I can't bring myself to say anything else.

"Shhhh…" She pats my arm as she always does when I'm upset.

"Darrell's here with her."

"Darrell?"

"Her husband."

"Oh. I have her purse and stuff." I manage to say.

"Ok. Let me see if I can get one of the nurses to bring them to her."

"Can I see her?" I want to see her. I need to see that she's ok, but deep down, I know she isn't. What would I say? What could I say?

"Not tonight, Baby, she's resting. She's not long come out of surgery."

"Oh." I say again, because I don't know what else to say. Surgery? My heart sinks further.

When I stand, a tall dark-skinned man is walking towards us.

Mr. Martin.

I recognize him from the pictures in her office. I guess they were able to get in touch with him.

"Thank you, Tameka."

I just stare at him.

"You saved Angel's life."

I begin to shake my head slowly. I want to tell him how sorry I am about the baby and that maybe if I'd driven a little faster I may have been able to...

"You saved my wife's life." He says as if he is admonishing my thoughts.

"But I—"

"No buts, God is in control, Sweetie."

God?

God.

Did God hear the pain that cut through Mrs. Martin? How could God do that?

I can't think about that right now. It's too much.

I hand him the purse, her satchel, and keys. When he turns to walk away, I stop him.

"Mr. Martin." I quickly close the distance between us and reach towards the leather satchel. I pull out the big brown envelope in the side pocket. He hands the bag to me without question. I start to pull out the folders.

"We were supposed to do these today. I'll take care of it."

He gives me a soft smile.

"Just keep everything in here. I'm sure she won't mind if you borrowed her bag."

I take the pretty leather satchel, place the envelope and folders back inside neatly, and pull the strap onto my shoulder.

I can do this. I will do this for her. It isn't much, but it's something.

CHAPTER 7

Normally my mom gives me a speech before she lets me drive off in her car, but not today. Today she just hands me the keys when I ask to borrow it. I pause before walking off, but when she only smiles and says, "Be careful," I gather Mrs. Martin's bag and head towards the door.

It's as if I've grown up overnight. Maybe I have. Maybe after seeing someone lose their baby it changes you.

I overheard my mom telling my dad that not only did Mrs. Martin have a miscarriage, but there was some other kind of damage as well and they had to do a full hysterectomy. I think that's when the doctor has to remove all of the parts that a woman needs to have a baby, but I'm not really sure. So, not only did she lose this baby, there is no hope of her having another. I don't want to think about that right now. I just want to get the folders done.

I park in front of Staples, not wanting to see or face Jessica at Stewart's. I just can't bear her sad eyes and especially her bulging belly, after everything that happened yesterday. A pang of guilt hits me because I know Jessica needs a friend, but I can't do it today. Monday maybe, but not today.

"I don't think I can get this one any bigger without losing the edge of this column."

"Let me see." When the guy from behind the counter spoke to me the first time his voice was so familiar that it took me a moment to reply, because I was wracking my brain trying to figure out what was familiar about it. I'm sure I've never seen him before.

"Do you see here?" He says, holding up the original next to the copy, breaking into my thoughts.

I look up at him and he's smiling at me. It's annoying because I want to smile back, but I don't think I should feel like being happy today.

"Umm." I look where he's pointing. "I think it'll be ok, it's the words that's most important."

"What kind of words do you like?" He asks, with way too much familiarity.

I look up at him and meet his eyes. They hold me in place for the briefest of moments. My heart starts racing. Why do I suddenly feel nervous?

I turn and glance over my shoulder. No one is there. Somehow my eyes slide up to meet his again.

My face feels warm. What's wrong with me? Then I remember he's asked me a question.

What was it?

"Uh… What?"

If he's disturbed by me acting and sounding like an idiot, he doesn't let on.

"Words. What kind do you like?" He repeats, smoothly.

What the hell kind of question is that? What is the deal with people lately, asking me these crap questions?

What kind of words do you like?

What does he mean? Big words? Small words?

Say something clever. Please brain, come up with something!

Then it hits me. I repeat something my PaPa used to say.

I say, "I like words that do not disguise the truth."

His eyebrows raise a fraction and he smiles.

He doesn't reply to my words just goes back to the copies.

When he has them all done, I ask if there's a workroom. There isn't, but he moves my things to another counter and says I can put my folders together there. He helps me spread everything out.

"If you don't mind me asking, what's this for?" He asks, gesturing to the folders and the enlarged assignments. So I tell him.

"Why are *you* doing them?"

My throat tightens and I try not to think about the previous day. "I'm helping someone out."

"Oh."

And for some reason, I don't want him to stop talking to me, even though I don't *want* to feel like talking. I know that's crazy but, maybe I'm teetering on the crazy line right about now.

"I'm wondering if there are some eye doctors in the area that would be willing to give free exams and glasses. Or just donate glasses for students who need them."

He just stares at me. He's probably trying to figure out if I'm sincere or crazy, who knows.

"I'm sure there are." He looks thoughtful and shakes his head. "You know, that could be a great community service project for college or just because it's needed."

"You don't think I'm crazy?"

"Why would I think you're crazy? It's noble and selfless. You should contact some optometrists in the area just to see how they could help."

I think about what he said for a few moments and wonder if I could really pull off something like that. Could I start a non-profit to help kids who need glasses? I've read articles about kids as young as ten who started all sorts of non-profits.

Maybe.

But for now, I need to get these folders done.

The guy begins helping other customers.

Who Am I

Who is this guy? I'm still irritated by my reaction to him. Then I start thinking about what exactly is my reaction to him?

He makes me feel nervous, but he also makes me want to smile for some unknown reason—even when I feel like I shouldn't.

His eyes are haunting. My hands are shaking.

I must still be upset about Mrs. Martin.

Yea, that's it.

I look up at him. Looks like he's copying some church programs and also giving someone the business cards they'd ordered.

I'm trying to concentrate on what I'm doing but, my betraying eyes keep straying towards Mr. What-Kind-Of-Words-Do-You-Like. I wonder how old he is. He looks about my age, though he definitely doesn't go to my school; I would've noticed.

A few guys have asked me out, but none have sparked my interest, let alone make my face heat and heart race.

But this guy… I want to respect the pain I'm feeling about Mrs. Martin and all, but I just keep thinking about how his voice makes me want to listen to every word he has to say. His eyes make me want to be the image he's looking at.

It really doesn't need to be said, but the guy is good looking—tall with pecan brown skin, but not too tall where he looks like a freak of nature. He's definitely better looking than Chase Thibodaux, who's supposed to be the hottest guy at school.

"My name's Austin if you need anything else."

Oh no! He catches me staring at him. I put my eyes and mind back on the folders, vowing to pluck my eyebrows out if I look at him again.

It takes me about forty minutes to get everything together and I can hear Austin is busy with customers. I stuff the last of the folders in the bag and am about to turn to leave.

"Hey, you done?"

I glance up briefly before pretending to adjust the folders in the satchel. "Yea. Thanks for your help."

"No problem." He slides a flyer in front of me. I look at it. It's for a place I'd heard of, but have never been—a place where the cool, trendy people kick it. And not the people who claim the "cool" title, but the ones who really are, because they are who they want to be and don't care what anyone else thinks about it.

"Have you ever been to 26?" He asks. It's a trendy café that hosts open mic nights for things like poetry and even local bands and singers.

"No." I say.

"You have to be eighteen to get in." He's fishing for my age, I can tell.

I say nothing but my heart is doing flips while my mind is telling it to calm down, it's just a flyer. I look at the paper. It's for tonight, spoken word open mic.

"It's pretty cool. You should come." When I don't say anything, he continues. "Poetry consists of words that tell the truth."

"I'm eighteen," I blurt out. It's all I can think to say. Is he asking me on a date or is he just telling me about the event?

"Then great. You should get there by eight to get a good seat." Someone wants him at the other counter. "I'll be right there." He calls over his shoulder and then turns back to me. "Eight o'clock at 26." He says through a smile that will be floating around in my head for days, and then he's off to help the customer.

What?

I pick up the flyer. What just happened?

Am I meeting him there with his girlfriend? Is he expecting me to come alone?

What...is...*happening*?

I carry the folders out to the car and wonder what to make of Austin.

Then it hits me!

How stupid can I be? He didn't even ask my name. I place the bag and flyer in the car along with thoughts of Austin. It's time to visit Mrs. Martin.

CHAPTER 8

The nurse tells me that Mrs. Martin's husband has gone to check on the girls. She's asleep when I get there, so I just sit in the chair next to her bed. There's a clear tube running from a bag of liquid on a pole to her arm—an IV, I think it's called. I watch it.

Drip, drip, drip…

She looks so…so vulnerable. Not like the strong confident woman I know from school, at all. The one who leaves fear in her wake—not because she's cruel or mean, but rather because everyone knows she doesn't play. Now, here she is lying quietly in a cloud of grief.

Who Am I

I pull out my phone to check my messages—no texts. I'm a little surprised my mom hasn't called or texted. I think she's trying to let go a little since I'll be leaving to go off to college soon. I'm sure she's at home worried and wondering if I'm dead in a ditch somewhere, so I decide to put her out of her misery.

```
Me: Hey ma...went to Staples @
hospital now. She's asleep.
Will stay for a bit and head
home.
Mom: Ok...cooking ribs and mac
today
Me: Yum!
```

Who Am I

I click off the text and surf Facebook and then as if my fingers have a mind of their own, I click back on the text.

```
Me: Ma are you using your car
tonight?
Mom: No… something you want to
Do?
Me: Yes, there's open mic
poetry nite at 26
```

There's a long pause before she replies.

```
Mom: Ok. Your dad says it's
fine as long as you're not out
too late. Someone going with
you?
```

Me: I'm meeting people there.

It's kind of the truth and I still haven't decided to go, but I figure I would check just in case.

"Hi Tameka." A sleepy voiced Mrs. Martin. I look up into her heavy lids, stand, and quickly move to the bed. I have no idea what to say to her. How do I tell her how sorry I am for not getting her to the hospital fast enough, for the baby, for...

"Mrs. Martin I'm so—"

"Be sorry for nothing, Tameka. Thank you for everything. You saved my life."

Her husband had said the same thing. I did nothing.

"But..."

"What did I say!" She snaps. And just like that, Mrs. Martin is back.

I tell her that I put the folders together and for a moment she just stares at me. She clears her throat and quickly brushes away a tear with the back of her hand. I pretend not to notice.

"Thanks." Is the soft strangled reply. I stay and visit with her for a while, carefully staying on safe subjects. We talk about what she wants me to do with the folders, because she'll be out a while. I ask her about the book they're reading for book club. She's hating it so far, because the characters are too raunchy. I immediately want to read it.

She tells me that she used to teach kindergarteners and how she hated singing all the little songs. It also bothered her that they could never make a straight line. "They wobble too much. It drove me crazy."

I laugh at this. I cannot picture Mrs. Martin teaching five-year olds. It turns out that she was better suited for high school and had actually taught calculus for about seven years. She's been an assistant principal for four years.

Her husband is a representative for an oil and gas company and travels a lot, so she spends much of her time keeping her girls busy. "I get to deploy my kinder teaching skills, after all." She says giggling a bit. Her daughters are five and six.

It's amazing how someone who's so emotionally and physically battered can somehow muster up the words to make *me* feel better, but she does. I kind of feel guilty about it, but even that wanes when I think of her strength.

Who Am I

A week ago if someone would've told me that I would be willingly talking to Mrs. Martin outside of school, I would've told them they were crazy. But here I am.

It's still a little weird, but it gives me a whole new perspective about teachers and principals. We think they are these creatures that live and breathe school, but they are just as fragile and vulnerable as the rest of us, with lives as complex as our own.

I hadn't planned on coming here, but find myself at Stewart's Print N' Copy. It occurs to me that I don't really have any friends. Trina and I used to hang out, but I never felt comfortable confiding in her about anything important. Or is it that I don't have anything important going on in my life worth discussing?

Today, I find myself needing a friend and even though we've been in different cliques for years, I'm hoping Jessica can be the friend I need.

She's at the counter as usual. I don't really know what I'll say, but here I am so I better come up with something. Jessica looks up and smiles at me, tentatively, but a smile nonetheless. She looks like she's about five or six months pregnant, not extremely big, but you can definitely tell she's pregnant.

She used to be my best friend. What happened to us? I've been thinking all this time that it was her who pulled away from me, but maybe it was me. Maybe I resented her for going off to private school— something that wasn't even her fault.

92

"Hey Tameka."

"Hi Jess."

Our greeting is cautious, both wary of the other.

A tentative step… on the edge of what?

Friendship?

"Need something copied?" She peers at my empty hands. "Or, are you picking up something?"

"Well actually I'm wondering if you'll come with me somewhere tonight."

Her eyes widen. She clearly wasn't expecting the question. "I…uh…"

"What time do you get off?" I fill in quickly.

"In about an hour."

"So will you go? I've never been there and I want a wingman—well a wing-woman."

93

"Where're you going?" I can tell she's interested.

"26."

"26?" She glances quickly at her stomach. "I…I can't."

"Why?" I ask, frowning.

"You know why." She whispers.

"I'm not asking you to go get high with me. We're just going to listen to some poetry." She giggles. "Come on." I urge. "You know you want to go."

"The question is…why do *you* want to go?"

My mouth twists trying to stifle a smile and I look away.

"Spill it, Tami! You only look like that when you're embarrassed about something and you're only embarrassed when there's a boy involved."

I'm touched that she remembers that about me and a little annoyed that she sees through me so easily. "So are you going to roll with me or not?"

"Tameka, I—"

"Jessica, being pregnant doesn't turn you into a freak."

"Tell that to my parents." Her eyes are suddenly extremely sad. "Why?" She questions me.

"Why aren't you a freak?" My forehead creases as I look at her.

"Why are you being so nice to me?" Anger flashes across her face. "I don't need someone feeling sorry for me. So what's the deal? We haven't hung out since we were kids and all of a sudden you're asking me to hang with you, like we haven't ignored each other for years."

"I need a friend." I say sincerely, and I mean it. "And at one time we were the best of friends and I miss it."

"So, you and Trina aren't cool anymore?"

"Not really. Long story, plus I don't think I've had a true friendship since we were little."

Someone walks up to the counter to ask for the code to the computer. She tells me she'll be right back. I look through the invitation book while I wait, sure my mom isn't going to hear me out when I tell her I don't want a graduation party. I wouldn't be surprised if she's already picked out the invitations.

"Ok." Jessica says softly, as she approaches the counter again. I smile in response and she asks, "Can you wait around a little while? I could use a ride home; my mom dropped me off this morning." I vaguely wonder where her car is, but determine it's none of my business.

"Sure." I say.

And there it is, a flame of anticipation flaring in my stomach as I think about the night ahead.

CHAPTER 9

We stop at Jessica's first, to let her grab clothes, check with her parents to see if it's ok for her to hang out for the rest of the day, and go to 26 with me. She says they won't care and she's right. They used to be so overprotective of her, but now, now they're just indifferent.

It's still incredible to me that we live in the same neighborhood, but never really see each other.

We walk back out to the car. Before getting in, Jessica says out of the blue, "I was their little princess in their perfect little world." She gestures to her belly and slides in. "Now, everyone knows we're just as fucked up as everyone else." Something in her tone causes me to turn to her; her features have hardened. "That's why they don't talk to me anymore. They figure if they pretend I don't exist… then… I won't." The last two words come out so softly, I almost didn't hear them.

She looks at me and her eyes fill with tears. "They treat me like I'm not even here. They don't talk to me, they don't look at me, and they damn sure don't acknowledge that I'm pregnant." She sniffs loudly and continues talking, but turns away from me. "They refuse to talk about it, like it's going to go away. It's not going to go away." Her voice gets louder with more than a hint of frustration and anger. "There's a baby growing inside of me and it's not going away!" She's practically screaming now. I just stare.

Who Am I

She glares at their house. "What am I supposed to do?" She screams and then suddenly softer, she says, "What am I supposed to do with a baby?" She stares into her lap. "I'm eighteen years old... I heard my dad tell my mom that he's tired of people whispering about me in the store and that he doesn't want me seen in there anymore." She waves a hand in the air. "There goes my job."

Jessica turns to look up at one of the windows in front of the house. "I'm not fucking invisible!" She screams again. "I'm a teenager with feelings and hormones raging out of control, who had no one to talk to about those feelings. Maybe if someone would've told me not to listen to all the bullshit a guy might tell you to get into your pants and that it's very possible to get pregnant your first time, then I wouldn't be in this position." Her voice changes to a mocking tone. "But of course there was no need for any of *those* kinds of talks, because we were the prefect family and in perfect families teenage girls who get pregnant happens to someone else!" She slams her palm on the dashboard. "But I *am* in this position, damn it, and it won't change." She slams it again. "I'm a girl who made a mistake… A mistake." She repeats, her voice lower this time, as if trying to convince someone of its truth. "That doesn't take away from the fact that I'm smart, I'm caring, and I'm strong!" Calming some, she adds in a steely tone, "I will not disappear and make this convenient for you."

I reach into the center console to pull out a McDonald's napkin and hand it to her. She takes it, wipes her face, and takes a deep breath. "Think they heard me?"

"No." I say truthfully with a sad smile.

We both laugh a sad, ironic laugh, breaking the tension and grief that hovers in the car. She'd been in the car when she began her tirade, so no one heard her, but me. But just as I'm about to back away, I see a curtain move in the upstairs window. They may not have heard her, but something tells me that someone felt every word she said.

In stark contrast, my parents are overjoyed to see Jessica and treat her like she's their long lost daughter come home. And just as promised, my mom has a big meal of ribs, macaroni and cheese, and green beans.

All of my favorites.

Even my dad is solicitous towards Jessica, encouraging her to eat a lot. "It'll be good for the baby." He repeats. It's like we're celebrating something. Though, I can't be completely happy, because it almost feels wrong when Mrs. Martin has suffered such a loss.

After we eat, we all go into the family room to watch television. My dad loves Sci-Fi, so he's sitting back in his recliner, instead of being in his shop fiddling with someone's motorcycle, or riding his. It really is like a holiday—everyone hanging out together on a Saturday afternoon.

Jessica is on the loveseat and my mom and I are both perched on the sofa with our feet beneath us. It doesn't take long for Jessica to doze. My mom's big meals have a way of doing that to you. I would've dozed too, Sci-Fi is not my thing, but instead, I follow my mom into the kitchen to help her with the dishes.

"I'm so glad to see that you and Jessica are friends again." My mom says as she hands me a plate to put into the dishwasher.

"You are?" I'm surprised.

"Yes. Why do you say it like that?" She frowns and scrubs some cheese off another plate before she hands it to me.

"Because I figured you would freak, because you wouldn't want me to hang out with a pregnant girl."

"She's not contagious, Tameka."

"I know, but…"

"I know what you mean. No parent wants to see their daughter in this situation. It's difficult for everyone, but I suspect she's having a hard enough time with her own parents."

"Yea," is all I can say.

"That bad, huh?" My mom always understands.

"Yea, they've been awful to her, and Mr. Stewart is about to kick her out of her job."

My mom shakes her head. "Some people will let pride destroy their only chance at happiness." She continues handing me the dishes and we don't say anything else until we're done.

"Mom…"

"Hmm?" She mumbles as she reaches to put away the flour in the top of the pantry.

"Thank you."

"For what, Hun?" She asks, still not looking at me.

"For being you." She turns then and really looks at me. I keep talking. "At the time, I hated all those embarrassing talks we had *con-stant-ly*, but I realized today that me knowing all that stuff, was your way of protecting me."

"What happened?" She pulls a chair out at our little dining table and I sit too.

"Jessica's mom kept her in the dark about all that stuff, and I think if she would've known...well...I think she may have made better choices."

My mom reaches for my hand and holds it gently. "And that's what it's all about, Baby. Making good choices."

"But how do we know which ones are the good ones?" I ask, really needing to know.

"The more we know about things, the better choices we make. But there'll be times that we still make, not necessarily bad choices, but maybe they're not the best ones for us."

"Then what?"

"Then that's when we find out what we're really made of."

"What do you mean?"

"I mean, it's what we do in bad or not so good situations that makes up our character. We learn what we're made of."

I immediately think of Mrs. Martin and her question: *What are you made of?*

"What about those people who always seem to do well? What about them?"

"First of all, what you see may not always be what's really going on. You never *really* know what's going on in another person's life. That's why you have to be good and kind to everyone. You never know what that person is going through, even if they appear to be happy and have everything going for them." She turns her head towards the family room when we both hear Dad snoring and she smiles. "He never makes it through an entire movie."

"Have you ever made bad choices?" I ask.

"Have I. Yes, Tameka, I have. I still do and will in the future."

"Really?" I'm surprised. She always seems to have it together all the time. She's always organized and making sure my dad and I are as well.

"Yes." She chuckles a bit. "Don't look so surprised. It would be hurtful for me to tell you that even when you make the *right* choice everything will be alright, but that's just not the case." She holds up air quotes when she says the word "right."

"So, why even try?"

"We try, because there's a chance things will go as we want them to, but if they don't, then oh well…" She brushes her hands together. "We dust ourselves off and start again." She reaches for my hand again and holds it firmly with both of hers. "No matter what, we get up and keep moving forward. We take the good with the bad and use both as lessons to keep us

109

humble enough to know that life will not always be perfect."

"But what about Jessica?"

"You be as good of a friend to her as you can and the rest will work itself out." She pauses a moment and then leans in a little closer. She looks so earnest. "Be a good friend, but don't lose sight of yourself in the process. This is Jessica's journey. There's nothing wrong with helping her along the way, but it is *her* journey."

"Ok, Mom." I'm not quite sure if I really understand all about the journey stuff, but I let it go for now.

CHAPTER 10

Austin was right; 26 does get crowded. This is my first time really going out so I'm not sure what to expect. The guy at the front checks our ID and gives us a wristband indicating that we're too young to drink, but mostly everyone is sipping on coffee anyway. I see a few people with wristbands. I also see some people drinking glasses of wine, I guess, but most everyone else has mugs of coffee.

I've never been in 26, and always wondered why it's named with a number. I look around after we enter. Every inch of the walls and ceiling are letters of the alphabet.

Ah…there are twenty-six letters in the alphabet.

There's book art all over the place. Repurposed pages of books turned into works of art. We find a table. The stage isn't so far away that we can't see anything, but it's far enough away for us to blend into the crowd.

Jessica seems to be a bit more relaxed. No one stares at her like she's a freak; in fact, a few girls ask her when she's due and if she knows if she's having a boy or a girl. I was right. She's nearly six months. She doesn't know what she's having yet, but according to what she's said to the last lady who asked, she's hoping for a boy.

Of course while I'm checking the place out, I'm discreetly looking for Austin.

"I'm sure he'll show up." Jessica says, nudging me with her shoulder.

Well, maybe not so discreetly.

We're sitting at a tiny little plain round table that doesn't look like it's big enough for two people, yet there are four chairs. Hmmm...intimate seating.

"I have no idea what you're talking about. I'm not looking for anyone. A guy told me about this event earlier today, and I thought we could come check it out. I needed a change of scenery." I reply nonchalantly.

"Well, check out the scenery that's walking this way." She's looking towards the bar area. I try to keep my eyes from going round. Austin and another guy are walking towards us and they both aren't bad at all on the eyes.

Who Am I

Austin smiles when he sees us and I don't know what to do. Should I wave, smile back…stare at him, and look stupid, which I'm sure I'm mastering perfectly at the moment. So, I quickly smile and wave. Not too enthusiastically, but just enough to let him know I'm speaking to him whether he's coming our way or not.

Oh please, please come our way.

And he does.

I glance at Jessica and she hits my leg underneath the table. "Who's that?" She whispers. "The tall one, is the guy I was telling you about and I don't know who the other guy is." I tell her, trying not to look like we're talking about them.

The guy walking with Austin is a few inches shorter than him, but just as good looking. He looks

114

Hispanic with a built-in tan, short curly dark hair, and exceptionally handsome. I see several females turn to look at them, but either the guys don't notice or don't care. I do notice that they both are wearing wristbands like Jessica and I.

"You made it." Austin says, as they walk up to the table and sit down like he's late showing up for our date.

Is he? Is this a date? Can't be. He doesn't even know my name.

I'm seated between Jessica and Austin and the other guy is on the other side of Austin, but since the table is so small we're all pretty close to one another.

Austin extends his hand across the table to Jessica. "Hi, I'm Austin and this is my friend, Gabe." He gestures towards Gabe and then he turns to me.

"Gabe, this is the girl I was telling you about, Tameka." I'm so shocked I don't know what to do. *He knows my name.* "Tameka, this is my best friend, Gabe."

"Hi Tameka." Gabe says and looks towards Jessica. They're waiting for me to introduce her, but I'm still stuck on *this is the girl I was telling you about.*

What was he telling him about me?

How does he know my name?

Somewhere in the fog of my confusion I hear Jessica say, "I'm Tameka's friend, Jessica. Nice to meet you." She speaks to them both, but her eyes never leave Gabe's and his seem to have the same problem.

Austin and I exchange a look. I momentarily forget about my anxiety about him, too busy being intrigued by the eye-play between Jessica and Gabe.

Jessica has always been beautiful to me, even when I

thought she was too full of herself.

Tonight, her hair is a mass of dark curls, giving

her an eclectic look that goes perfectly with her white

peasant top and multicolored flowered skirt. Her

smooth dark face is free of make-up, but she's still

easily the prettiest girl in the place. Gabe is in a trance.

I wonder how the revelation of her pregnancy will

change his reaction to her.

The guys settle in at the table with us like we'd

planned to meet there. I, however, have no problem

with this. I just wish I knew what to expect from the

evening.

My normal routine is going to school, maybe

even a school function, and hanging out at home. Trina

and I used to go to the mall and movies sometimes, but that's about it.

Now, here I am sitting in a trendy night spot with a boy I'd only met a few hours ago, ordering lattes in a place where they sell alcohol, and have live entertainment.

I am totally out of my element.

CHAPTER 11

Who am I?

I think about that question, in which I still don't believe I can answer, as I sit back and wait for the first poet.

Her name is Lilly Lane. A tiny little thing that looks like her voice will never get above a whisper, with short blond twists in her hair, and round glasses that are way too big for her face. She looks about my age or maybe a year or two older. I don't know, but she looks young.

"Wait 'til you hear her." Austin leans over to whisper to me. "She's phenomenal."

Who Am I

I was in the process of thinking that this must be her first time here, because she looks so shy and overwhelmed by all the people staring at her. So I'm taken aback when Austin knows who she is.

I am also reeling from the feelings fluttering in my belly from his close proximity to me. What's that all about? It isn't like I've never been around cute guys before.

When my cousin was at school with me last year, I used to hang out with him and his friends all the time. They're all good looking, but somehow this is different. There's never really been a guy that made me want to give him my attention, but Austin...I not only want to give him my attention, I want his as well.

So far we've all just been casually talking about the things that teens normally talk about—future plans, who's the hottest new music artists, and work. Of course I can't indulge in the work conversation, but Jessica and Austin have lots of work complaints in common, since they both work in the printing world. Gabe, like me, doesn't work either. He's a senior at a high school across town. Austin, I find out, graduated last year.

Before I can dwell anymore on our evening so far, or reply to Austin, Lilly begins to speak. Well that's not an accurate description of what she's doing. It isn't so much that she's performing an original poem, I feel like she's exposing power.

Her words come out in great rushes like waves and you either ride them or get swept under.

Whoa! Spoken word poetry is powerful.

I'm transfixed. This small person possesses the power to capture all of us and take us on…what, exactly? Her poem is about the rain. Well, that's not quite right. It's about a single drop of rain and its journey.

It's as if I am that drop. I feel its struggles, its determination, its single mission, and reason to exist. She ends the poem with the drop landing on a little girl's hand, way before the other drops fall, which causes the little girl to look up.

"Stay prepared…for whatever..." Lilly urges. And at that moment she looms so large I have to blink a few times.

She *is* good. I am still transfixed as she continues.

"You never know when you'll have to get there before the rest, in time for someone to look up… so they can come in from out of the rain in time." She ends.

A hush penetrates the room for a few heartbeats before the entire club pushes it away with loud handclaps, whistles, and finger snapping. She walks off the stage transforming back into a quiet ordinary female, from the powerful voice of …I don't know what.

I clap along with everyone else, but my eyes, in a daze, follow Lilly as she walks so unassumingly back to her seat. People from nearby tables, pat her arms and back.

Who Am I

As I watch her, I know without a doubt, that she's a raindrop that falls first. She knows who she is; why don't I?

CHAPTER 12

We listen to a few more poets, but none move me like Lilly. Will I ever be the type of person who could help someone? I wasn't much help to Mrs. Martin, I hadn't even been a good friend to Jessica, and wondered if I'd ever been a friend to Trina.

Trina. It's like we'd never been friends at all. I don't miss her nor does it bother me that she hasn't spoken to me since the incident in the lunch room.

Will I ever be the first raindrop?

"Come with me to the restroom, Tami." Jessica mouths to me as the MC is about to introduce the next poet. I lean over to tell Austin we'll be right back. He nods his head and point in the direction where the restrooms are. I'm grateful because I don't have a clue where they are. I give him an awkward half-smile, because I don't know what else to do as Jessica and I stand.

I notice the surprise in both Gabe and Austin's eyes. Jessica doesn't and I'm glad. I'm a little annoyed by their reaction to her baby bump, but quickly get over it.

Of course they're surprised. We'd all been talking about high school and it being our last year so they had no reason to expect her to be pregnant.

Before we walk away I see Gabe mouth the words, "Awe shit."

That does annoy me.

I glare at him, but he's too busy staring at Jessica to notice. I do, however, notice that he looks very sad. As we turn towards the ladies room, I turn back to our table and see Gabe whispering something to Austin.

"Oh my God, Tami, they're sooo cute!" Jessica exclaims as soon as we step beyond the restroom door. "Did you set me up on a blind double date?"

"If I did, then it was blind for me too." I laugh. "Seriously though, I just met him today, he showed me the flyer, and said I should go. I came and now he's sitting there like we've made these plans for weeks."

"Gabe is so nice." She states dreamily

We both reach a stall at the same time. She continues her chatter about Gabe. I refuse to talk and pee. That just seems so...so...so rude and invasive.

As we're washing our hands I look in the mirror and the person staring back at me looks pretty and confident. I usually don't pay much attention to my hair or a mirror except for brushing it into a ponytail and making sure I don't have crust on my face. Tonight, I took the time to curl my hair with my mom's big rollers and I'm pleasantly surprised by the results.

My hair falls in soft waves to my shoulders and under the glaring fluorescent lights of this restroom, the natural bronze highlights make me feel…well… like I'm looking kind of hot! I turn to make sure my jeans are fitting as cute as I feel they are. I'm wearing my favorite jeans and a light blue top that shows off my shoulders. Yep…I'm definitely looking hot tonight.

Jessica hands me a paper towel. "I wish I would've met Gabe before this." She says pointing at her belly. A cloud of disappointment shadows her face. "But, there's no changing things now. My little bumble bee is on his way, whether I'm ready or not." The disappointment changes to happy anticipation. And it dawns on me that in spite of the way her parents feel, she's happy about her baby.

We hadn't really talked about it. I guess, because this was a kind of first date for us too. We're on the verge of getting to know the older, newer versions of us.

I understand what Jessica means by the comment she makes about Gabe, but I can't be a true girlfriend if I don't try to look on the bright side of things and tell her he might be different. Then I change my mind and decide to go with the truth.

"I have no idea how guys feel about dating pregnant girls, especially ones who they didn't get that way." I toss the paper in the trash near the sink, fluff my hair a little, something I never do, and turn to look at Jessica. The door opens and three girls walk in. We all do the polite "hi" and smile.

"Come on," I say. "We'll talk about it later." As we weave through the tables back to ours, I can't help but ask, "Is it Justin's?" Justin had been her longtime boyfriend, until recently. I wonder casually if the baby broke them up. Jessica nods at my question and rolls her eyes, as if saying she wishes she'd never met him.

I have perfected girl-eye-rolling and speak it fluently. So, I know exactly what Jessica is saying with her facial expression.

Bastard.

Fine as he is, I always knew he was a loser.

She shrugs her shoulders and I shake my head letting her know that I understand. I briefly speculate what the guys' reaction will be when we return to the table, especially Gabe's. Will they treat me or Jessica any differently now that they know she's pregnant?

And then, I suddenly don't care.

They are nobody to us. We didn't know them before today and I imagine Jessica and I will be just fine if they suddenly drop out of sight. Which is very possible, pregnancy or not.

They both smile as we return to the table.

"We were going to order you another latte, but didn't want them to arrive before you did, and you think we'd put something in your drinks." And before

131

either of us could respond, Gabe added, "We both have teenage sisters and give them the 'don't leave your drink unattended' speech before they go out."

Just then, a waitress appears. Austin looks at us with a question in his eyes. I nod and turn to Jessica. She nods as well. Gabe pipes in again, "They have great herbal teas, Jessica." She smiles and nods her head quickly agreeing to the tea instead of the coffee.

I think I saw on TV that herbal tea is better than coffee for the baby. I guess Gabe knows something about it too, for him to make the suggestion.

Thoughtful. Hmmm...

"Give her the sweet apple tea," Austin addresses the waitress, but looks to Jessica for confirmation. I guess he's the table spokesman. She nods again and then he just gets the rest of us the same round of coffees we had already. Before the waitress turns and leaves, Gabe stops her to add something else, but I can't hear him. I'm too busy thinking how grown up all of this feels.

"Having fun?" Austin asks.

That smile. Oh my.

"Yes, I'm glad you told me about it."

"I had to think of some way to see you again." He says, coolly.

I hope the floor is clean, because my heart just popped out of my chest and fell onto it.

Say something clever…say something clever, Tameka.

"Why would you want to do that?" I settle for honest versus clever, because frankly, that's all I got.

"You really *don't* remember me, do you?"

133

Blank stare.

What's he talking about? I've never seen him before today.

"What do you mean, remember you?" My mind is racing trying to explore all the corners of memories that could have included this good looking guy. "We've never met before."

When I say the words, his smile falls a bit, and he sighs.

What in the world can he be talking about? I don't remember him at all. In the background I can hear a very angry woman on stage who must have been used and mistreated by every male human that has crossed her path, because she's cursing the male population with every other syllable.

"We've met before?" My voice squeaks with the question.

"Yes, and I was sure I would never see you again and cursed myself for not getting your number. And then you showed up in the store today."

I'm thinking that he still hasn't asked for my number. He just took a chance that I would show up here. But, I'll get back to that thought soon enough.

When did we meet?

He's wearing a nice black t-shirt and when I ask him again about meeting him previously, he pushes up the sleeve of his left arm and turns his bi-cep towards me. My hand flies to my mouth and my eyes widen.

On his arm is the coolest tattoo of a guitar entwined with musical notes. I've seen that tattoo before. I immediately know that we have indeed met.

My eyes shoot to his and his face lights into a grin.

"See, I told you."

CHAPTER 13

It had been a dare. My cousin Flora dared me and her sister Sheryl to ask these two guys at the corner store if they would give us a ride on their motorcycles. It was during spring break of my junior year and the three of us were headed to the beach in Galveston. It was Flora's car so she was about to pump gas and Sheryl was going to go inside to pay. I was in the backseat trying to find my other sandal so I could get out too.

Flora was still upset that she'd chosen a dare during a game of "Truth or Dare," the night before. We'd made her text Chad Phillips and tell him that she would go on a date with him. Chad was crazy about

Flora and had asked her out several times, but he annoyed the heck out of her and she had never agreed to go. The text said that she would go out with him. So, needless to say she was still pissed.

One of the guys on the motorcycles had gone into the store, but his friend was waiting for him on his bike in the parking lot.

"I knew you two wouldn't do it." Flora whined.

She was trying to come up with something to get us back for her dare.

"Girl, we don't even know them. At least you know that Chad won't take you in the woods and cut you into pieces." Sheryl shouted, slamming the car door.

"You sure about that?" Flora threw back at her.

While they were arguing, I had my eye on the guy on the bike. His helmet was black with a shaded visor so I couldn't see his face. He wore a gray t-shirt and blue jeans. All I could see was his pecan-brown arms from the sleeves of his t-shirt. The rest of him was covered. He wore gloves so I couldn't even see his hands, but his shirt had the word "Nevermore" in the shape of a raven on it.

I love that poem, "The Raven," and figured that any guy who was familiar with anything about Edgar Allan Poe, couldn't be all bad—even though Poe was such a freak.

Flora finished pumping the gas and followed her sister inside. I slipped on my other sandal and hopped out of the car too. But instead of following them, I walked over to the guy on the bike.

"Hi, would you give me a ride on your motorcycle?" His head tilted for a moment and I tried in vain to see through the tinted visor. I couldn't see his face at all. I guess he was looking at me, but I really couldn't tell. He scooted up a bit and waved me on. I was surprised that I wasn't even nervous and it didn't occur to me that jumping on the back of a bike with someone was completely insane.

I got on, he started the bike, and we were off. He drove fast, or maybe it just seemed that way, because I'd never been so exposed on the street before. Here he was, covered nearly from head to toe and I was wearing some short white shorts, sandals, and a halter covering my bikini top. I leaned into his shoulder with my cheek pressed against him, and held on around his waist.

The sleeve of his t-shirt flapped wildly in the wind and I noticed that he had a tattoo on his upper arm. I couldn't really see it, because the wind was in my eyes. I don't know why I hadn't grabbed my shades. What was I thinking? All I could do was shield my face with his shoulder.

The roar of the engine, the security of his back pressed against my front, along with the intoxicating smell of his cologne, was a mind-altering blend.

"You ok?" He yelled above the noise of the engine and wind.

"Yea!" I shouted back. Though I'm not sure if I was. I'd never been so intimately close to a guy and it was, well…making me feel kind of tingly.

But I'm sure my hair was a scary mess, which was quite sobering. Good thing it was in a ponytail, but

I could still feel the edges framing may face like a sunbeam. Good grief!

I noticed he was making the block around the store. At the traffic light, I took the liberty of lifting his sleeve a bit so I could get a better look at his tattoo. It was a guitar entwined with music notes. It looked as if it was dancing.

"Nice tattoo." I whispered to myself.

"Huh?" He asked turning his head around to try to see me.

"Nice tattoo." I repeated, louder this time.

"Thanks."

"Do you play?"

"Every chance I get."

And before I could say anything else, we were lurching forward and then we were turning back into the store parking lot. His friend was waiting for him and my cousins were gaping at me like I had two heads.

"Thanks!" I yelled to him, trying to be heard above the rumble of the engine.

"No problem." He shouted back. Sounding a bit muffled from the helmet.

I jumped off and was headed back to the car.

"Hey!" He called to me. "What's your name?"

"Tameka!" I yelled and quickly climbed into the backseat of Flora's car. If he said anything else, there was no way I could hear him, because my cousins were all teenage-girl-screeches and very loud. While they were busy telling me how crazy I was and that they couldn't believe I actually did it, I was looking out the back window wondering who Mr.

"Nevermore," really was.

CHAPTER 14

"You're Nevermore." I breathe. Though it's difficult to get the words out, because my throat is closing with this startling revelation.

"What?" His brows knit together.

"That day...that day on the motorcycle...you had on a shirt that said, 'Nevermore.'"

"I did?" He looks as if he's trying to remember.

"It was the reason I decided to do the dare. I love that poem."

"I was a dare?"

My cheeks heat. I guess I shouldn't have mentioned that part.

But why not?

I need him to know that I'm not the type of girl who just runs off with strange boys on a whim…even though that's exactly what I did. "Yea." I reply quietly.

"What was the dare?" He sounds amused.

"My cousin dared us to ask you and the other guy if you would give us a ride on your bikes."

"I figured it must've been something like that."

He's grinning again, so I guess the dare doesn't bother him. Austin pulls out his phone and before I can question what he's doing, he looks up at me expectantly.

"What?" I ask, confused.

"Your number." He says. "I'm not letting you walk away again, before I get it."

He wants my phone number? My teeth sink into my bottom lip trying to hold off the goofy smile threatening to take over my face.

His face falls. "You got a man?"

Trying to play it cool and not look like my insides were screaming, *hell no I don't have a man,* I nonchalantly shake my head "no."

"So, can I have your number?"

I give it to him and he punches it into his phone. I feel my phone vibrate in my pocket and reach for it.

"That's me calling you so you can program me in."

"K." I pull out the phone and add a new contact. "What's your last name?" I ask him.

"Bailey. And yours?"

147

"Cummings." I tell him and smirk.

"What?"

"I should put you in as 'Nevermore.'"

"And I should put you in as 'Miracle.'"

"Why?"

He absently pushes a sugar packet around in little circles on the table near his spoon. "Because it's a miracle that I've met you again." His voice is low and people are clapping again, but I hear every word. "You have no idea how many times I went back to that store, hoping to see you again." He adds.

I don't want to tell him that that was the first and last time that I'd ever been to that store—so, I don't. We only stopped, because it was the last exit before we got onto the bridge to take us to Galveston.

After the show is over the guys walk us to my mom's car. I see Gabe and Jessica pull out their phones and I assume they're exchanging numbers. I lift a brow at this.

"He really likes her. What's the deal with the baby's father?" Austin asks me.

I roll my eyes.

"Like that?" He seems to understand immediately.

I lean my back against the driver's door and Austin stands in front of me. Not too close, but close enough for us to look like we're speaking privately. I pull the key from my pocket. I hadn't wanted to bring a purse tonight so I just have a single key, my phone, license and money. Speaking of which, the guys paid for our tab at the table. That was new. The whole night feels like a date.

"I don't want you to put me in your phone as 'Nevermore.'" His face is sincere and his voice has a light, but serious edge to it.

My mouth tilts into a half-smile, "Why not?"

"It sounds so negative. He didn't see his Lenore anymore and I want to see you again." He reaches for my hand and gently takes it in his, leans over to my ear and whispers, "and again."

All traces of humor gone, the breeze of the new spring night holds promises of something good to come, and I'm inclined to believe it.

Austin gives my hand another soft squeeze and for the first time in a long time, if ever, I'm looking forward to tomorrow.

Yes, this is really feeling like a date. The *end* of the date... Anticipation blossoms, bold and bright within me.

He tilts my chin to look up at him. His eyes hold mine—that smile. That smile makes me want to be that raindrop—strong, confident, and necessary. And not for him...for me.

"In a few weeks, maybe I'll be in your phone as 'Babe.'" He says, pretty sure of himself.

I cock an eyebrow. His confidence is not lacking—I like that.

"Like the pig?"

He laughs loud enough to make Jessica and Gabe turn to look at us.

"What are y'all talking about over there?" Gabe asks.

"Tameka was just telling me about a movie we're going to watch in a few weeks."

I laugh then.

"Do you ladies want to go to IHOP?" Gabe asks us.

"That would be fun, but I promised my mom I wouldn't stay out too late. Plus I have church in the morning?"

"Rain check?" Austin asks, looking hopeful.

"Sure."

"What church do you go to?"

"East Mount Olive, on Spencer."

"I've been there before." He states.

"Have you?"

"Yea, but it was a long time ago."

"Well…" I say, fiddling with my keys.

"I'll let you go." He says, not moving away.

Oh goodness, the end of the night. Will there be a kiss. It isn't really a date…but… Maybe it is a date. And before I can complete another thought, he gives me the sweetest, softest kiss possible. It isn't my first kiss, but it may as well have been. The other few cannot compare.

When he pulls away, I try to clear my glazed daze to speak. There's something I just have to do. I lift the sleeve of his shirt and trace his tattoo with my fingertip. "Do you still play?"

"I'll be playing forever."

I smile, and I don't know what it is but boldness pushes my feet onto my toes and I lean in to give him a quick kiss and then duck into the car. Jessica climbs into the passenger seat still making goo-

goo eyes at Gabe. I make a face, give Austin a quick wave, and drive off.

Jessica's phone pings.

"The guys want us to let them know when we make it home."

"OK."

She looks at me, I glance at her, and we both erupt into giggles, knowing we'll be up well into the night talking about our evening at 26.

CHAPTER 15

Jessica decides she wants to go home. She isn't quite ready for the piercing eyes of the judgmental "Christian folk," as she calls the members of my church. So I drop her off before I head home, but we text for about an hour after we're both settled into bed.

It turns out that Gabe is interested in her and was worried, at first, that she has a boyfriend. He doesn't seem to mind at all that she's pregnant and thinks Justin is a prick for leaving Jessica when he found out.

I wonder idly if his feelings will change once she has the baby or when she becomes huge and grouchy. Will he still want her knowing she's carrying another guy's baby?

All this stuff rolls around in my head, but I hear my mom's voice and decide that it's none of my business, because this is her journey and not mine. I have my own issues to worry about. I'm trying to place all the foreign feelings I'm having about Austin, so I don't have time to dwell on what's happening with Jessica and Gabe.

After saying goodnight to Jessica, I place my phone on the nightstand and switch off the lamp. The darkness does nothing to shut off my mind. I am giddy with thoughts about Austin and a little freaked out that he's the guy on the motorcycle from so long ago. My cousins and I still laugh and talk about that day and I have to admit that at times I've wondered about him. Of course I can't go back so I don't dwell on it.

I'm really looking forward to getting to know him. I haven't learned much about him except that he rides a motorcycle or did at one time; he plays the guitar and apparently likes poetry. Oh yea, and he works at Staples.

Plus he is fine... fine... fine!

I pull the blanket up to cover my shoulders as I nestle into my pillow. My phone pings and lights up. I thought for sure Jessica would be knocked out by now. I start to leave it until morning, because I really do need to get to sleep. My mom doesn't play about getting up for church.

I reach for it anyway.

It's Austin. I pull myself up and rest my back against the headboard, unable to keep the smile from my face.

Austin: Are you up?

Why do people ask that? If you weren't up then you would definitely be up after the text goes off.

Inside I am screaming: *YES, I'M UP AND SOOOO GLAD YOU TEXTED ME BECAUSE I'VE BEEN THINKING ABOUT YOU SINCE I LEFT 26!* But instead of sounding like a lunatic I reply:

Me: Yes, what's up?

Austin: Can I call?

Me: Sure

My phone rings almost immediately. "Hey." I say when I answer.

"Hey." He repeats. "I was hoping you would still be up."

I slide from the headboard back onto my pillow trying to cocoon myself in the blankets and Austin's voice at my ear.

"I'm up." There's a pause so I rush to fill the empty space. "I had a good time tonight. Thanks for telling me about it. I think Jessica may have a crush on Gabe." A tinge of guilt heats my cheeks for throwing my friend slightly under the bus just so I can have something to say.

Still he says nothing.

"Hello." I panic. Did I lose the call?

"I'm here."

"Oh. I thought I'd lost you." And as soon as the words leave my mouth I wish I could grab them back. That sounded so desperate.

"No, I'm here."

Silence.

Ummm…did he just call me to hold the phone? I hate when guys do that. Well, that one guy that I went out with briefly last summer.

"So…what's up?"

"Do you know how many times I've dreamed of you?"

Whoa! I was not expecting that. My face is in full-on grin mode.

"Have you?" I whisper.

"Yes, and after a while I tried to convince myself that you were just a figment of my imagination." There's silence again and all I can hear is the whirling of the fan above my bed. What do you say to that?

"And then, today, there you were." He continues. "My dream girl."

His dream girl?

Do boys talk like this? Should I be worried that he's some sort of super stalker? Is his room full of pictures of me pasted on the walls?

Hmmm...I guess not, since he hasn't seen me since the beach day last year.

I watch too much Criminal Minds with my mom.

"I'm no dream girl." I murmur.

"You're my dream girl." *What? Is he for real?*

"Why were you looking so sad when you came in the

161

store today?" He asks in a less stalker-ish tone, seeming to sense that he's getting close to sounding on the left side of creepy.

"It's a long story."

"I've got time."

So I tell him the whole sad tale.

"Why were you in the assistant principal's office?"

"I'll save that for another day."

"Ok." He chuckles and then there's a pause again. "I can't believe I'm talking to you?"

"I feel like that too."

"Do you?" He asks, sounding surprised. "I figured you'd forgotten all about that day."

"No."

"So you remember our ride?"

Who Am I

"Every single moment." I answer quickly in a soft tone that's foreign, even to my own ears.

I can almost hear his smile through the phone, which triggers one to spread across my face.

This weekend has been a hell of a rollercoaster ride.

"So what are your plans for after high school?" He asks me.

Finally. Normal conversation.

"I want to go to Lamar University in Beaumont. I want to go off to school, but I really don't want to be too far away from my parents. I'm that rare kid who actually loves to be around her folks. Plus I have an aunt who lives there and has promised me free home cooked meals."

"You're going to Lamar?" He sounds surprised.

"Yea. I know there are a lot of schools here in Houston, but like I said, I want to go away and test my wings, so to speak."

"Do you believe in serendipity?"

"Strongly." What guy talks about serendipity or even knows what it is? "Why do you ask me that?"

"Tameka, I go to Lamar… Well I did."

My eyes fly open. He goes to Lamar?

"See, we're meant to be together."

"You go to Lamar?" I ask, to make sure I heard him correctly. "But why aren't you in school? Do you come out here to work on the weekends?" I'm excited and crushed at the same time. If he's just here on the weekends, that means I won't get a chance to see him that often. Assuming he would want to.

"Actually, I took the spring semester off." His tone changes from one of excitement to forlorn. "My mom has cancer."

Oh no. I can't even imagine how I would feel. "I'm sorry."

"Thanks, but she's better now. After Christmas, we thought we were going to lose her, so I took off from school to spend more time with her."

I think about what I would do in that situation and agree that I wouldn't want to be that far away from my mom either, if she was sick like that. "She was pissed when she found out I left school." He continues. "But right now she's almost back to her old self and insists that I 'get my behind back to school.' I started working at Staples to get out of the house, plus I needed to either be in school or working. I'll return to

Lamar in the summer, but I'm not sure what I'll do in the fall. My dad says I can always go to U of H and work with him."

"I'm sorry about your mom, but I'm glad she's doing better." My voice, low and sincere. "I can't believe we may be at the same school next year."

"Told ya, it's fate."

I don't know how to reply to that. So I don't.

We talk for about an hour more, before common sense kicks in, and tells me I better get to sleep. It's after 2:00 am. I've learned that he still has his motorcycle and promises me a ride. He's also very heavy into music. He plays not only the guitar, but base, and violin.

I'm stunned.

Who Am I

What young guy in our crazy generation wants to be a music composer for films? He's different, that's for sure and he likes me. He really likes me and I don't have a clue what major I want to study. I don't have a clue of who I am.

I feel so inadequate. What can he possibly see in me? I want to ask him, but I'm afraid his answer will be just an idea of who he thinks I am and not an accurate picture of me. He's had a lot of time to wonder about me and conjure up all sorts of ideals.

Austin has so much to offer and I wonder if I can even measure up?

CHAPTER 16

I make it through church without my head bobbing and I am extremely grateful for Rev. Samuel's very long prayer after the offering and the short sermon. After church, I gobble down some leftovers and make a straight line to my bed for my famous after church nap.

My phone is still on silent from church, so I didn't hear the text that came in from Austin about ten minutes ago.

Austin: Do u want to hang out?

Suddenly I'm no longer sleepy.

Hang out? Doing what?

Only one way to find out…

```
Me: Sure. What do u have in
mind?
Austin: Take a ride with me.
There's something I want to
show you.
Me: On your bike?
```

I wonder briefly how this will go over with my dad. He's a motorcycle guy and all, but dads' tend to have double standards when it comes to their daughters, boys, and motorcycles.

And again, there's only one way to find out.

```
Austin: Yes. I have an extra
helmet. Wear jeans and
something on your arms.
Me: Ok.
Austin: 30 min?
```

Me: Ok

I give him my address and run downstairs to talk to my dad. I figure if I have his blessing then my mom will follow more easily. He's watching the Sci-Fi channel again and is close to dozing in his recliner.

"Dad is it ok if I go for a ride with a friend of mine?" He lifts a sleepy eye at me. He must see something in my facial features that makes him focus a bit more clearly.

"Who's the friend?" He asks, turning the volume of the TV down with the remote. I inwardly roll my eyes.

"His name is Austin." I look back at him trying to appear as casual as possible.

"Austin?" He repeats, tilting his head to the side, appraising me.

"Yea. I met him about a year ago and just saw him again yesterday." It's partly the truth; although I'd never officially met Austin.

"Where you going?"

"I'm not sure."

Dad stares at me for a long time.

"Ok, Tameka. Be careful."

I smile at him and can't help giving him a quick hug and a kiss on his cheek. I love my dad. He's such a great guy. He's always been fair and not too overprotective, though I know he'll hurt someone if they harm me.

I fail to mention that Austin will be arriving on a motorcycle. I plan to rush out the door the moment I hear him drive up.

Who Am I

My hair is still somewhat tame from last night. It was church worthy, so it should be fine for Austin. I briefly worry what it'll look like after it's smashed inside a helmet and then I don't care. I'll get to hold on to Austin while we fly through the streets of Houston, wherever we're going.

As I'm picking up the pile of jeans off my bed to stuff them into the closet until I come home, I hear him drive up. I run to the window and to my horror, he's getting off the bike and walking to the door. I grab my sweater from the floor, slip on my Chucks, and run downstairs—careful not to kill myself in the process.

Too late. Dad is opening the door. Austin just would be the guy that greets parents.

Jeez. This guy!

"Hi, Sir. I'm Austin Bailey. I'm here to pick up Tameka." He extends his hand to give my dad a handshake.

"Hey Austin!" I call from the bottom of the stairs, trying desperately to get out of here before my dad can stop me from going off with some dude who rides a motorcycle. They both turn to look at me. Austin smiles and my dad's forehead creases as he turns back to Austin.

"Bailey?" He asks Austin, still gripping his outstretched hand. "*Austin* Bailey?"

"Yes, Sir." Austin replies—his brows starting to bunch too.

"Are you Dr. Bailey's boy?"

Austin grins. "Yes, Sir, I am."

Who Am I

My dad pulls Austin into the house patting him on the back. He closes the door. I stand dumbfounded watching the scene unfold in front of me. Apparently my dad knows Austin's dad.

Dad turns and yells into the kitchen, "Pat!" still gripping Austin's hand. "Pat, come out here a minute!"

He finally releases Austin's hand and grips one of his shoulders. "Let me look at you." He says appraising him. "You've grown into a fine young man."

My mom comes out drying her hands on a kitchen towel. She looks at me and then she sees Austin. She looks up at my dad wide-eyed with her face full of questions.

"Pat, look who it is." He turns back to Austin. "Little Austin Bailey. Ed's son."

Who Am I

Ed?

What in the world? How's it possible that my dad knows Austin? Then that word comes back to me.

Serendipity.

"Oh my gosh!" Gushes my mom and she pulls Austin into a hug. Austin looks at me as if asking "What's happening?"

When she lets go, my dad says to me. "Tameka, you and Austin used to play together when his dad and I were doing some work on his office building." He turns to Austin. "You two couldn't have been more than three and four."

Austin's eyes find mine and I can read, "See, I told ya," plainly in them.

My dad sees the bike out of the open family room window. "That your bike, Son?"

"Yes, Sir."

"Aww, he's so polite." Mom gushes again. I roll my eyes and is ready to be away from this…this…whatever is happening.

"Your dad was always into bikes too. We've worked together on a few. And if I remember correctly, you've been riding since you could barely run."

"That's about right." Austin replies.

"Well, it sure is good seeing you. How's your mom and dad?" Dad pauses a moment, frowning. "Seems I recall someone saying that your mom was sick a little while ago. How's she doing now?"

"She's much better. Gave us a scare, but the new treatments seem to be helping."

"We'll be praying for her." My mom says, reaching for his arm and squeezing it gently.

"Tell Ed you met his classmate, Charlie Cummings."

"Ok, I will."

"Oh, I could tell you some stories about Ol' Eddie Bailey, before he became, Dr. Bailey." Austin and my Dad laugh and I feel I'd better put a stop to this before my dad gets going really good.

"Ok. Dad, Mom, we're headed out now. I won't be out too long."

I grab Austin's hand and drag him out the door. He twists around to turn and wave with his free hand to my parents who are hovering in the doorway.

His dad is a doctor. He's handsome, funny, has a great personality, and knows exactly what he wants out of life.

Why is this guy single?

I stand in front of the same bike that I rode a year ago.

It's weird. Like déjà vu, but better.

Austin hands me his extra helmet. I put it on and climb on the back of the bike with him. I turn to see my parents still there. My dad is grinning, but my mom looks a bit apprehensive. That's more like it. It was starting to weird me out that they are so ok with me riding off on motorcycle with a boy.

"Hold on tight," he says over his shoulder.

Oh you don't even have to worry about that.

And we're off.

"That was weird back at the house." I say over the engine noise. We stop at a stop sign and he turns to look over his shoulder.

"Not to me."

"It wasn't?"

"No." There's a car pulling up behind us. He lifts his feet and turns on the cross street. I wonder where we're going. "We've known each other for fifteen years."

This guy.

I just have to ask. "Why are you single?" I yell over the wind and engine noise.

"I'm not." What the hell! He's not? "My girl and I met fifteen years ago!" He shouts against the wind. My arms tighten around his waist. Why fight it?

CHAPTER 17

I don't pay attention to where we are going, so when we pull up behind an office building, I'm surprised. I anxiously wonder if he's trying to find a secluded place to kiss me. The building sits on a piece of property all by itself and apparently it's closed, because there are no cars in sight. The back of it sits close to a canal and is separated from it by a chain-link fence. There are other buildings like it on either side, but there's no connecting driveway.

"What is this place?" I ask when he pushes the kickstand down and removes his helmet.

"My dad's office."

I wonder why we're here and hope he doesn't think he's getting me alone so we could uh…

"I know you just met me, but don't worry. I just want to show you something."

"Ok." I breathe, relieved. I guess my concern is plain on my face. I can feel my cheeks heat from embarrassment.

He sits and waits for me to ease off the bike. Dang, my butt is sore. It takes me a few steps to get my legs moving easily again. I pull off my helmet and hope my hair doesn't look as bad as it feels. I reach up and feel it plastered to my head.

"You look fine." He says reaching for the helmet.

I roll my eyes, because I know it's a lie.

I hear the approach of a vehicle and look up to see a little red Beetle coming our way. "Who's that?" I ask as I watch the car come to a stop.

"My dad."

I raise an eyebrow at this bit of information and try in vain to tame my hair. This is getting interesting.

"Dr. Bailey?"

"Yes. Who your dad apparently knows as Eddie." Austin smoothly gets off the bike and places my helmet on the seat of the motorcycle. "And no…my dad doesn't drive a little red Beetle. That's my mom's car."

I don't respond to that, because I'm watching the tall older copy of Austin stride towards us.

"You must be Tameka." Dr. Bailey says extending his hand to me. I shake it firmly and look him in the eye like my dad taught me to do, but I'm sure my puzzlement is displayed all over my face.

Why are we here and why am I meeting his dad? And what has Austin told his dad to make him know my name?

"Yes, Sir. Tameka Cummings. We just found out you and my dad know each other."

"You're Charlie's daughter?" He asks with a wide grin taking over his face that is so much like Austin's.

"That's me."

"Well isn't this a small world."

He looks at Austin, "Boy did you know that Tameka used to boss you around when you were kids?" Austin turns accusing eyes to me.

I throw up my hands in defense. "Don't look at me. I have no memory of that."

Dr. Bailey walks to the back door and opens it. "Austin told me about what you want to do and I think it's great. I'll do whatever I can to help." He says holding the door open for us. "And that was even before I knew you were Charlie and Pat's daughter."

Austin stands to the side to let me walk in first. What's his dad talking about? I'm so confused. I walk in and then I get it.

Dr. Bailey is a doctor of optometry.

The glasses.

He leads me to a huge box in a storage area. "Well here they are. We collect old glasses to be recycled. They're all yours."

"What?"

I look from Dr. Bailey to Austin. What am I supposed to do with them?

Dr. Bailey tries to explain. "Austin told me that you wished somehow you could get eye doctors, like myself, to donate exams and glasses."

I just stare at him. I don't remember telling Austin that, but I guess I must've. "But I don't know anything about how to go about that." He waves me to a stool at a small counter in the room and I sit down. Austin has disappeared for the moment. "It's just that one of the assistant principals at our school has been enlarging homework assignments for some of the students and I thought it might be easier or better for them to have glasses." I explain to him as I absently pick up a pair of glasses from the box and place them back. "She told me that many couldn't afford them or didn't qualify for the exams and or the glasses."

"So you wondered if doctors would donate their time for exams and help with glasses?"

"Yes." I agree and nod. "I know it's probably much more difficult than it sounds."

"Not really." He shrugs. He smiles gently at me and places some sort of contraption near where I'm sitting. It looks almost like a microscope. "Most times, all it takes is for someone to care enough to ask and organize a plan."

I just stare at him again. Can it really be that easy?

"There's not too many kids your age who would even care, let alone, try to do something about it." He smiles at me and then begins fiddling with the knobs on the microscope thingy. "Says a lot about you, Tameka."

What? What does it say about me? That students having glasses will prevent me from going to the print shop to make copies for them?

"You care." He says while reaching in the back of the machine with a small screwdriver. "This thing just needs a few adjustments and it'll be good as new."

I was lost again.

"There we go." He turns some knobs and stands in front of me. "We need more young folks to care about each other. So if you really want to take this on, I'll help you. This dinosaur right here," he pats the microscope looking thing, "is called a lensometer. It determines the prescription of a pair of glasses, and I can teach you how to use it."

At that moment I know that I will do whatever it takes to try to help. What if my parents couldn't afford glasses for me? What would they do? He says that the hardest part is getting things organized. I'm Pat Cummings daughter, I can do that.

"How do I get started?"

Just then, Austin walks in with a few more pairs of glasses and places them in the box on the counter. He looks expectantly at me and a little apprehensive. "Was this a good surprise or do you think I'm lame for dragging you to my dad's office?"

I beam at him. "I think it's pretty cool."

Who is this guy and where has he been for the past fifteen years? I feel like I've known him all of my life and not at all like we just met yesterday.

CHAPTER 18

The next six weeks or so, fly by. It's like my entire life has changed since that day in Mrs. Martin's office. She's back at school today and I'll be glad to see her back in her office or patrolling the halls in her killer heels.

While she was out, Mrs. Martin had made arrangements for the teachers to give me the assignments on Friday afternoons and I've been getting them enlarged over the weekends—at Staples of course, because true to her dad's word, Jessica no longer has a job at her dad's store, and I refuse to patronize the shop now. Plus when I go to Staples, I get to see Austin at work.

Who Am I

I asked my mom if Jessica could move in with us, because the tension at her house was stifling. My parents agreed, but Jessica refused. She said that she didn't want to bring her problems to us.

After a while, though, her Aunt Francine insisted she move in with her. She had never had any children and Jessica is her only niece. From what Jessica tells me, she treats her better than her mom ever had. That surprises me, because I always thought the Stewarts were the perfect family.

My dad lets her work in his real estate office helping the receptionist. It isn't much, but it's something.

Oh yea, it turns out that Gabe thinks Jessica is cool and all, but his parents doesn't want him dating a pregnant girl. Unfortunately he hasn't gone against their judgment, so he and Jessica no longer talk. She says she's ok with it, but I'm not sure she really is. She really liked him.

It turns out that I have a lot of help with the "glasses project," which is officially called Helping Students with Vision (HSWV). I'm in the process of creating a non-profit group to help students in high school get glasses—with the unwavering help of my mom, Mrs. Martin, Dr. Bailey, and a couple of teachers at school.

The school board has recognized my efforts and gave me an award a week after I presented the idea to them at a board meeting. Of course there's still lots of work to get it up and going, but a few students who have current prescriptions or who have lost or damaged glasses, received some of the donated glasses already.

I've been working with Dr. Bailey after school most days and he's been showing me how to take the old glasses and determine their prescription. The whole world of eyes is quite fascinating to me. He says I really have a knack for. I've met several other optometrists and ophthalmologists in the area who are actively helping me with HSWV.

Two months ago I was hanging out with Trina and just existing. Now, I feel so productive…like I can conquer the world. How can so much change in two months?

I watch the last of the students leave the building heading for their cars, their ride out front, or to the buses. Of course I will not be riding the bus today. I'm sure Austin is already outside waiting for me.

We're on our way to the University of Houston to finish filling out our paperwork. While working with Dr. Bailey and his staff, I've discovered that I have a passion for working with people and making sure they have healthy eyes. It's been sort of an informal internship. At any rate, U of H is impressed with my volunteer hours and my desire to be an optometrist or maybe even an ophthalmologist. I haven't decided…and that's ok, because I have a plan for both paths.

Unfortunately, more cancer was found when Mrs. Bailey went in for her last appointment and Austin refuses to go away to school. He will be continuing his study of music at U of H with me. I can't help but smile when I think about what a great guy he is and how we really do seem to be destined to be together.

Yesterday he told me he loves me. He said he'd waited as long as he could to tell me, as to not freak me out. Apparently, he wanted to tell me the night we were at 26, but didn't want to risk running me off.

I think about all of this as I stand outside of Mrs. Martin's door. She's been gone six whole weeks and it's Monday. The last time I stood here, I had to rush her to the hospital. I quickly push that memory away.

So much has happened since then.

I think someone must be in her office with her, because I can hear muffled voices. I straighten the hem of my pink blouse and brush away some lint from my navy slacks. And just like before, I find myself softly kicking the floor with the tips of my shoes—navy flats that match my pants. Am I nervous? I push one side of my hair behind my ear and take a deep breath.

The door swings open wide, startling me, and Shay Jones, of all people, walks out with her face all balled up. She looks at me and throws daggers my way. I smile sweetly. "Hello to you too, Shay."

For some reason, I can't possibly fathom, she ignores my greeting and runs out to catch her bus. I laugh, loudly.

"Come in here, Tameka!" Jeez, does this woman not miss anything?

I walk in. Mrs. Martin is sitting at her desk lining up the stapler with the tape dispenser. She's wearing a soft lime green suit with a white blouse and a skirt that matches her jacket. She looks…well…she looks like Mrs. Martin—sharp, professional, and stylish.

"Sit please." She's all business.

I do.

"Well?"

"Well what?" I smirk.

She cocks an eyebrow as if to say, girl don't play with me. This is the Mrs. Martin I've missed. She gives me another pointed look when she feels I'm taking too long to respond.

I'm ready.

I sit up in my seat, take a deep breath, and meet her eyes.

"I think it will take the rest of my life to try to tell you who I am, or even to figure out who I am.

What I do know is, who I'm not. I'm not someone who backs down from a fight when there is a fight worth fighting." She smiles at that. "I'm not someone who turns my back on a friend when my friend is in need. I am not a quitter. I'm not a coward. I'm not always perfect. My entire journey will determine who I am and I'm just at the beginning of it. But I am definitely not the same person I was when you first asked me that question…and I will be forever grateful."

Mrs. Martin leans back in her chair with her lips pressed together. She takes a deep shaky breath and nods her head.

Dear Reader,

Thank you, thank you for taking this journey with Tameka and me. This book is so special, because I love working with teenagers. In doing so, I see great potential in all of them. Sometimes, unfortunately, they don't or can't see what I see.

When Mrs. Martin asks, "Who are you?" it causes Tameka to slow down, take a moment, and really look within herself. Sometimes all it takes is for teens and young adults to focus on what they are doing with their time and how they are treating others. These two important things say so much about all of us. I challenge you to take the journey inside the mirror and discover what you're made of.

Happy Reading,

Natasha Simmons

nsimmons@nkwordflow.com
www.nkwordflow.com